Favorite Fairy Tales

The Wizard of Oz

Retold by Rochelle Larkin   **Illustrated by Lea Kaster**

The Playmore/Waldman® is a registered trademark of Playmore Inc. Publishers
and Waldman Publishing Corp., New York, New York

The Playmore/Waldman Bug Logo® is a registered trademark of Playmore Inc. Publishers
and Waldman Publishing Corp., New York, New York

Once upon a time a little girl named Dorothy lived with her kindly aunt and uncle on a farm in Kansas. Dorothy's only friend was her little black dog, Toto.

A terrible storm came and Dorothy and her aunt and uncle went to hide in a cellar under the ground. But Toto jumped away and ran into the farm house. Dorothy ran after him.

The house went up into the sky, and to a magic place called Oz, on top of a wicked witch. Only her silver slippers were left!

Suddenly a good witch magically appeared. She told
Dorothy to take the silver slippers and put them on her feet.

"But I don't want the magic slippers," Dorothy cried.
"I just want to get home."

"To find your way home," said the good witch,
"you must follow the yellow brick road to the Emerald City.
There the great Wizard of Oz can grant all your wishes."

Along the way Dorothy made three friends—
Scarecrow, who wanted a brain, the Tin Man who
wanted a heart, and the Cowardly Lion who wanted
courage.

But a wicked witch made great trouble for them.

Once she made poison flowers
to put them all to sleep.

But the good witch made a snowstorm. It destroyed the poison flowers and the friends woke up.

Evil flying monkeys helped the wicked witch capture Dorothy and her friends.

But Dorothy spilled water on the wicked witch, and she melted clean away!

Dorothy and her friends were once again on their way to the Emerald City.

NOBODY HOME

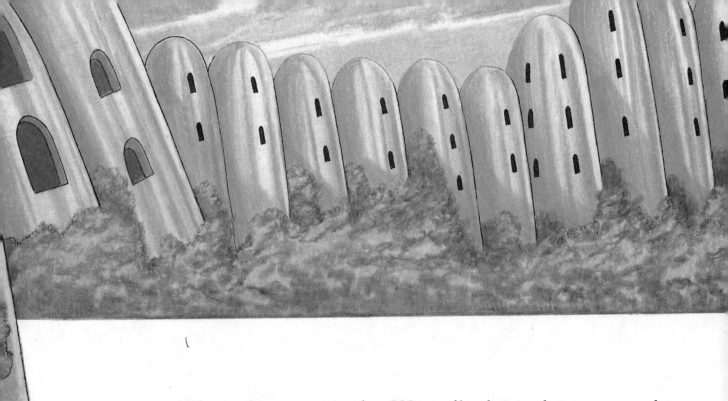

When they got to the Wizard's door, there was a big sign posted: NOBODY HOME.

Dorothy banged on the big door knocker.

"Go away! Go away!" said one of the Wizard's helpers. "Can't you see the sign? Nobody home!" The Wizard could be difficult. But Dorothy banged again.

At last the Wizard himself came to shoo them away.

"Go away! Go away!" he said. "No time! Don't bother me! Bye-bye!"

"No," said Dorothy, "we won't go away! We've been waiting a long time to see you. We even got rid of the wicked witch so we could see you."

The Wizard was impressed with that news. "Come in
and I'll see what I can do for you," he said at last.
"I want a heart," said the Tin Man.

"Hearts can be broken," said the Wizard. "But I will give you one that will last forever."

"I want a brain," said the Scarecrow.

"It's not *having* a brain that counts," said the Wizard. "It's *using* your brain."

The Wizard stuffed the Scarecrow's head full of pins and needles.

"There, now you have the sharpest brain in town," he said.

" I want courage," said the Cowardly Lion.

"Here," said the Wizard, handing the Cowardly Lion a green bottle. "Drink this!"

"Inside the bottle is courage," explained the Wizard.

"Courage always comes from the inside. Drink this and you will have courage inside you too."

The Lion drank and then pounded his chest. He felt very brave.

"I want to go home," said Dorothy.

"But my dear," said the Wizard. "You don't need me for that. You have the magic slippers. All you need to do is click your heels together and say your wish three times."

Dorothy held Toto tightly in her arms. She said good-bye to her friends.

She clicked her heels three times, saying, "I want to go home. I want to go home. I want to go home."

When Dorothy opened her eyes she found herself back safe in Kansas with her aunt and uncle. She hugged them tight and told them all about her magical adventure in the land of Oz.